STACKED DECK **FALLING**
Times/Up

Marty Begonis

Copyright © 2020-2021 Marty Begonis~
All Rights Reserved.

STACKED DECK FALLING
Times/Up

MARTY BEGONIS

marty.begonis@iCloud.com

Copyright © 2020-2021 Marty Begonis~
All Rights Reserved.

STACKED DECK FALLING

Welcome

I started to write down something one day and saw it wasn't that hard to jot down a thought or two.

It's now accumulating as I try to find more time I never really had in the first place.

I live in Vermont and have a small farm, beef cows, pigs, chickens & a 3 year old chocolate lab that keeps me from chilling out on a couch.

I'm a PitMaster as well, I love to cook bbq in my smoke house. Along with a big garden, mowing the lawn, repairing the house, sheds, fence, chores & fixing broke stuff.. well who's got time to write..

I only leave the farm if I absolutely have to & always a surprise when I get back.

Since CV19 a lot of people are stuck at home, feeling like there going crazy & most of us will be feeling that way before it's done.

My mother loved to read, always said she should write a book. But never did. She always hummed the music of her time never the words. Too bad because she had a beautiful voice & it was very comforting.

I also wanted to give a special thought about my father who never missed a days work, he showed me respect, honor & integrity. To work hard & be who you are.

So the books I write, I dedicate to my parents. Because as a teenager I put them through hell.

My books are my feelings, opinions & a true grit attitude towards what I see going on in the country during this rabbit hole era. With poems, stories & lyrics that I wrote about everything since January 2020 continued into 2021

Copyright © 2020-2021 Marty Begonis~
All Rights Reserved.

STACKED DECK FALLING

Paper walls ~

Speaking of the speaker's speeches
Brings up more stuff than #45's impeaches

What president now alive
Would they be talking about Amendment #25

Passing laws as fast as the virus grew
Who's pulling who's strings & who's pulling you

Fake media's tentacles whirling about
We're inside of a hole looking out

Believe this & won't show that
It's on all these networks it must be a fact

What's next in line, to become the past
Lurking about behind the blue mask

Stacked deck castle of cards
Calling in the national guards

Claiming victory before it's completed
Reality is they will be defeated

Copyright © 2020-2021 Marty Begonis~
All Rights Reserved.

STACKED DECK *FALLING*

Shuffled Deck ~

House of cards needs a flick
Knock them down cause they're all sick

They built their empire with deceit
Took this country from under our feet

This game was rigged from long ago
Fraudulent election of an imposter you know

Bring out a new deck
Keeping their hands in check

You know we all know what we saw
Win loose or draw

STACKED DECK FALLING

Governor~

All about his greed inside
An uncomfortable elevator ride

I'm the governor & I rule
You know you want it because I do

Covid count must be accountable
Ventilator black market non refundable

Christmas vacation with his family
Closings mandatory for you & me

Church's Schools Restaurants shut down
Because the governor is really a clown

20,000 missing vaccines when there was plenty
Hospital cruise ships are still empty

Corruption is unforeseen
Extortion is too extreme

Legalized abortion rates
Now the fetus faces fate

Made a fortune in money & fame
But as a governor he's pretty lame

He himself he idolized
Never sorry he doesn't apologize

Moving up in his pay grade
Grants himself another raise

He lashes out showing a temper
So nobody asks questions & they whimper

True Christian morels torn
Then another baby's death is born

Copyright © 2020-2021 Marty Begonis~
All Rights Reserved.

STACKED DECK FALLING

Go no Go ~

Some who claim to teach are a class act
Kids miss their friends & that's fact

This is just another strike, longer than the past
You donkeys ass get to class

Fool's play shutting church doors
Let prayer back in during these times of horrors

Out to dinner is therapy
Maybe later, catch a movie

What about medical care how's that been
Waiting forever to be seen

If someone young or old & unfortunately died
We are told it was all Covid, but they lied

Copyright © 2020-2021 Marty Begonis~
All Rights Reserved.

STACKED DECK FALLING

Mask competitors ~

Who's winning you don't have to ask
Team # displayed on their mask

Suddenly femininity masculinity
Competing masculinity femininity

Man not woman v/s Woman not man
Come to the game & see if you can

Years of training & funded generosity
Grilled day in day out therapy

There's a new game, a competitive fight
Talking about disparity of day & night

The game on way has a unique kind of spin
Throw away fairness & win

Women & Men equally can compete
Everyone's chance at an Olympic seat

Of course there's exceptions of sort
Until they make a separate trans-sport

Copyright © 2020-2021 Marty Begonis~
All Rights Reserved.

STACKED DECK FALLING

Vanished ~

Flue flue where are you
Will you be back in 2022

Will they give credit where credit is due

You've been here before again & again
Always came back through family & friend

I'm sure you'll be back & won't say when

But like Covid motivated politics
Corruption's skin is deep & thick

You're gonna be back & you make me sick

Copyright © 2020-2021 Marty Begonis~
All Rights Reserved.

STACKED DECK FALLING

No brainer ~

Basement of the president elect
Remodeling for a special effect

Stage hands hand over an oval stage
Sit at the desk & open the page

Signing executive orders, it's so insane
Colored pens keep him entertained

While he was coloring his ABC's
Vp is in meetings now overseas

This whole things really crazy though
Where's Biden, does he even he know

STACKED DECK FALLING

Digital Curtain ~

Imagine yourself in a word of electronics
It consumed your world it was so supersonic

Let's make it smarter than you & me
Hook line & sinker, we think we're free

Technology now a digital life a human forfeit
Influenced by politically motivated corporates

Camera & video are the tools
It's every station those scripted fools

America's 1st amendment they want to cease
Speak now or forever hold your peace

Copyright © 2020-2021 Marty Begonis~
All Rights Reserved.

STACKED DECK FALLING

Falsified ~

Everyone's death is from Covid

Fear from Covid

Suicidal incidents were Covid

Pneumonia from Covid

Old age was from Covid

Car accidents & heart attacks, yup Covid

People lost jobs & homes, again Covid

School kids miss their friends & hate Covid

Darn election was stolen using Covid

But there's one thing to appreciate about Covid

The speaker's face is covered from Covid

Copyright © 2020-2021 Marty Begonis~
All Rights Reserved.

STACKED DECK FALLING

Joe Crow rising ~

There's a new kid in town & the name is Crow
Hanging around just waiting on Joe
Because of the liberals in bungalows
Lucky lady in the political lights
Or a demonic angle
In the big lie, yes the big lies
Joe Crow warning every afternoon
Dive on into socialism, completely through
Into the blue blue blue
Ain't for me but it's ok for you
I see our country's burning
Cities are all on fire
Peaceful no they are a liar
Don't go out & don't you roam
Stay there at home
Parking garage to park your cars
You pathetic avatars
It's what I think & I'm not alone
Not alone no I'm not alone
Media's big money madness
Four years of gladness, turned to sadness
Not so surprising
Well it's a Joe Crow rising

Copyright © 2020-2021 Marty Begonis~
All Rights Reserved.

STACKED DECK FALLING

Puppet Clowns ~

China's using our politicians as puppet clowns

Big brother sees you while you're sleeping

They know the woke won't wake

They know who's trying to do good

And that Biden's on the take

Oh better watch out

With all the rioting about

Unicorns don't fly

Cause they don't exist, that's why

They're making a digital list

Analogs changing doubling it twice

Whatever they're doing I know it ain't nice

China's using our politicians as puppet clowns

Copyright © 2020-2021 Marty Begonis~
All Rights Reserved.

STACKED DECK FALLING

Richer or Poorer ~

The rich get richer & the poor get poorer
Now that they have opened this door

Rolling along together & working progressively
Small businesses doing successfully

Suddenly we feel a powerful earthquake tug
When right from under us out comes the rug

Everyone's caught by total surprise
Whoever did this we've come to despise

Living nightmare sees daylight
Somehow has managed to stay out of sight

Close down a perfectly thriving economy
Somehow We didn't see that coming anomaly

Nobody saw it coming but an elite few
They planned & schemed an evil brew

As they gloat with a cheshire smile
A verdict comes down from supreme judicial trial

Raging riots twice as before
As America shouts shut the front door

Copyright © 2020-2021 Marty Begonis~
All Rights Reserved.

STACKED DECK **FALLING**

Dig my brother ~

Only you & I know how deep is this fox hole
We scratched our grave as like a mole

I wait & so does my brother
Anxiety raged inside one an other

Hands clench our weapons of might
Vision of horror before the fight
Blasting light
Do we say good night

Dirt in mouth I search about
I don't dare to shout

We're both alive & we kinda smiled
I think of my brother once in a while

Copyright © 2020-2021 Marty Begonis~
All Rights Reserved.

STACKED DECK FALLING

Unrepentant ~

I treat everyone equally as I'd like to be treated
I say what I think, voicing our opinion is needed

I ain't wearing one, two or three masks
You ain't sticking nothing up my nose or my ass

And I'm happy with the pluming I got
Man I am & a woman I'm not

I ain't gonna get the shot neither one or two
Even after we see how it effected you

You try to take my gun
You won't see the next setting sun

However we got to this place we're at
You got into office, now your wallets fat

A square inside a circle, you try to place
Now the whole things a disgrace

Long waits the woes of the silent
This continues, it could get violent

Copyright © 2020-2021 Marty Begonis~
All Rights Reserved.

STACKED DECK — FALLING

Hark ~

Are we descendants of the angelic ark
Test tube genetics did they embark

Angels were different although they took an oath
Male & female & both

Some forgot why they were here
Then greed moves in using cancel fear

Totalitarian common cense laws
Indoctrination of insanity & all its flaws

At energies expense they wield their bliss
Power lessoning hit or miss

Weeding themselves out during a power grab
Canceled like us, now ain't that sad

Raging battle of stupidity & mights
40 days & 40 nights

Now that they have opened this door
Good will weigh in through a fog of war

Copyright © 2020-2021 Marty Begonis~
All Rights Reserved.

STACKED DECK FALLING

Critical race theory ~

Whole lot of mojo
It ain't no joke
We gotta wake the woke

Get the looters off the street
They won't stop until their beat
Then replace the speaker's seat

Liberals systemic lies spread fear
Massacres will suddenly appear
Just as new gun law restrictions get near

Secretly sweeping under the rug so profoundly
Reality of what's happening all around this country
Changing all the rules, putting it bluntly©

I've always been who I've been
I know clearly what I've seen
We need to escape their unicorn dream

Be it all as it is
It's only a movie & that's show biz
I know it ain't raining, their taking a wiz

Copyright © 2020-2021 Marty Begonis~
All Rights Reserved.

STACKED DECK FALLING

Endemic ~

Covid will always be
You don't know it cause we can't see
You want to wear masks go ahead but not me

Liberalism is the virus they spread
#46 stumbling around with an empty head
The outcome of it all we'll shortly dread

Animated caricatures, they target by voice
Stricken from the pencil & paper of choice
Banned books, movies & even the toys

Where we are is not the same
Where we're headed looks too lame
We're gonna have to step up in this game

Copyright © 2020-2021 Marty Begonis~
All Rights Reserved.

STACKED DECK FALLING

Covidicated ~

Sorry for your misunderstanding
Sorry for the mishandling

Brought on this pandemic
And all the crap that's so systemic

Learning nothing schools are closed
More restrictions again proposed

Believe nothing churches are forbidden
The real agenda seems to be hidden

Own nothing with jobs restrictions
No outlook for any ending predictions

Forget the possibility
Of them seeing reality

Should be a investigation
On all the new legislation

Copyright © 2020-2021 Marty Begonis~
All Rights Reserved.

STACKED DECK FALLING

Two sides ~

Brother against brother
They fought against each other

Arguing with out remedies
Families against families

The patriotism each of us favors
Neighbors against neighbors

Speak against it, you'll get some frowns
Towns against towns

We don't like the crap we see
Soon in time historians would agree

This country's in such a state
Reaching a peak of hate

This great storm, cold & muddy
Soiled great landscape separated & bloody

Just when you're thinking you're fine
Rain upon your moment in time

Build up the fire though in the boiler
Leaving an open door on the southern border

It's taken them time to re-arrange
Created a Trojan horse called Change

STACKED DECK **FALLING**

Double deal ~

Dirty double deal you
You're homeless with your family
Very sad but very true

Didn't matter if you voted or not
You ain't got nothing
What you get is what you got

That's what they want for you
Dependent on their stimulus candy
No mind of your own too

If you're working for the rich boss
They got a new kind of whip
Cancel culture, now you're lost

Waking up to what's going on
Looney tunes with a new cast
What made America seems to be gone

Americans have suffered the cost & more
Slipped in while we where content
Is this all not an act of war

Copyright © 2020-2021 Marty Begonis~
All Rights Reserved.

STACKED DECK **FALLING**

Two castles ~

One brother invests in stocks & doubles his savings
While the other must pay bills using his savings

One brother has a huge luxurious home
While the other rents a small house to own

One brothers kids get tutoring with nothing to lack
While the other the kids schools closed fall back

One brother orders food online with extra cash
While the other uses up their food stash

One brother sends his children to college
While the other ones kids miss the knowledge

One brothers children investing with great leaps
While the others kids are out on the streets

One brother says to the other that's how it goes
While the other says & that's what you chose

Copyright © 2020-2021 Marty Begonis~
All Rights Reserved.

STACKED DECK **FALLING**

Corona vaca ~

Your paychecks what 2400 + a month
When we stayed working you had fun

While you collect siting on your ass
We pay 300 month in extra tax

Stayed working all through
Got a lesser paycheck than you

In Vermont we just got a 9% tax increase
For your check & you sign a time share lease

Not to mention that we had to work
Essential worker without the perk

It's a nice vaca
Until you too have to pay

What's that about what you say
When they collect the taxes, you didn't pay

While you went out to eat
We had freezer burnt meat

But now I'm saving money I may have lost
Because with an empty freezer you turn it off

Copyright © 2020-2021 Marty Begonis~
All Rights Reserved.

STACKED DECK FALLING

Lightning Jane ~

White lightning
Ain't frightening

So inviting
Buzz tightening

Well we ain't fighting
White lightning

Oh & Maryjane is just the same
Long ago it became

Smoke the stuff you'll be tame
May ack stupid may act lame

Shit goes down you ain't to blame
Start off tomorrow just the same

Copyright © 2020-2021 Marty Begonis~
All Rights Reserved.

STACKED DECK FALLING

Pulling my train ~

Well my trains been running for some time now
Been around every bend
Up & down every mountain
And I made it home somehow

Saw the colors of the season's
They still leave me in awe sometimes
Never the same but always alike
Everything has it's reasons

Wondering what tomorrow will bring
Inside deep way deep in my heart
It'll all eventually work out
Until then I have my song to sing

Iron rolling on iron going down the track
The power of heated moments
Director of destiny my life traveling delights
I wanna keep going & I won't look back

STACKED DECK FALLING

Delusional reality ~

Everyone's in a majestic awe
What was not seen we just saw

Seems that we've been fooled
A socialistic scheme has been ruled

Tormented heart aches
Endlessly time waits

Touch an angel by heartfelt thought
Protection is what you sought

Journey your path however long
Keep your memories & you can't go wrong

STACKED DECK FALLING

Life experience ~

So what didn't you learn
Is it more time that you yearn

Things that happened you had no control
Was there anyone around you could console

When young did you ever cry
See a sad thing & you didn't know why

The present you got, not what you want
An inner anger that begins to taunt

Be patient & enjoy your youth
Too soon you'll know the adult truth

Before too long & around the bend
You're running on borrowed time The End

Copyright © 2020-2021 Marty Begonis~
All Rights Reserved.

STACKED DECK **FALLING**
Times/Up

Author

Author, Artist, Farmer & PitMaster
American hard worker living to support the dream of my great grandparents journey from Poland to America in their quest for a better life..

MARTY BEGONIS
marty.begonis@iCloud.com

Copyright © 2020-2021 Marty Begonis~ All Rights Reserved.

Made in the USA
Middletown, DE
16 February 2022